ROSE'S MAGIC TOUCH
by Nina Alexander

Illustrations by
Catherine Huerta

Spot Illustrations by
Rich Grote

MagicAttic Club

MAGIC ATTIC PRESS

Published by Magic Attic Press.

For more information contact:
Book Editor, Magic Attic Press, 866 Spring Street,
P.O. Box 9722, Portland, ME 04104-5022

First Edition
Printed in the United States of America
1 2 3 4 5 6 7 8 9 10

Magic Attic Club is a registered trademark.

Betsy Gould, Publisher
Marva Martin, Art Director
Jay Brady, Managing Editor

Edited by Susan Korman
Designed by Cindy Vacek

Library of Congress Cataloging · in · Publication Data
Alexander, Nina
Rose's Magic Touch / by Nina Alexander:
illustrations by Catherine Huerta, spot illustrations by Rich Grote.--1st ed.
p. cm.-- (Magic Attic Club)
Summary: On another adventure through the mirror in
the magic attic, Rose assists Peter Presto, world-famous magician, in an
internationally televised performance in Salzburg, Austria.
ISBN 1-57513-106-4 (hardback). -- ISBN 1-57513-105-6 (paperback)
(1. Space and time--Fiction. 2. Magicians--Fiction) 3. Salzburg (Austria)--Fiction 4.
Austria--Fiction. I. Huerta, Catherine, ill. II. Grote, Rich. ill. III. Title. IV. Series.
PZ7.A37785Ro 1997   (Fic)--dc21   97-28008   CIP AC

As members of the
MAGIC ATTIC CLUB,
we promise to
be best friends,
share all of our adventures in the attic,
use our imaginations,
have lots of fun together,
and remember—the real magic is in us.

Alison   Keisha

Heather   Megan

Rose

Table of Contents

Prologue

When Alison, Heather, Keisha, and Megan find a gold key buried in the snow, they have no idea that it will change their lives forever. They discover that it belongs to Ellie Goodwin, the owner of an old Victorian house across the street from Alison's. Ellie, grateful when they return the key to her, invites the girls to play in her attic. There they find a steamer trunk filled with wonderful outfits—party dresses, a princess gown, a ballet tutu, cowgirl clothes, and many, many, more. Excited, the girls try on some of the costumes and admire their reflections in a tall gilded mirror nearby. Suddenly they are transported to a new time and place, embarking on the greatest adventure of their lives.

When they return to the present and Ellie's attic, they form the Magic Attic Club, promising to tell each other every exciting detail of their future adventures through the mirror.

Chapter One

A MUSICAL AFTERNOON

W hat's this one called, Grandfather?" Rose Hopkins asked. She leaned back in the easy chair and closed her eyes, letting the music from the stereo speakers wash over her.

"It's the overture from an opera called *The Magic Flute*," her grandfather said. "It's by Mozart."

Rose opened her eyes and gave the

elderly man a playful look. "I figured it was Mozart," she teased. "You never listen to anything else."

"Not true," her grandfather protested with a laugh. "I love all kinds of music. Even that stuff you and your friends listen to."

You and your friends. Rose closed her eyes again and smiled. *You and your friends.* She liked the sound of that. She still could hardly believe how much her life had changed recently, when her parents decided to enroll her in public school instead of the private school she had attended since kindergarten. At first she thought she would never fit in at her new school. Then she met Alison McCann, Heather Hardin, Keisha Vance, and Megan Ryder. Rose wasn't sure she was going to like the four girls at first. But an amazing adventure in a very unusual attic had changed that. Now all five girls were well on the way to becoming fast friends.

"They're coming over any minute, you know," Rose said. "My friends, I mean."

Her grandfather reached for the control knob on the stereo and turned down the volume.

"I know. Your mother told me before she left for the library." He winked at his granddaughter. "She wants me to keep an eye on the lot of you."

Rose's mother was a graduate student and her father was a college professor. They had busy schedules, so Rose often spent time with her grandfather after school. She loved listening to his stories about their Cheyenne heritage and teaching him to use the family's computer.

"Maybe we should be keeping an eye on you," Rose said. "After all, you're the one playing the loud music."

Her grandfather laughed and turned up the volume again. But Rose heard the peal of the doorbell a moment later, even above the soaring notes of violins and oboes.

"They're here!" Rose jumped to her feet and ran to open the door.

"Hi, Rose," chorused Heather, Keisha, and Megan.

Rose greeted them and stood back to let them in. "Where's Alison?" she asked.

"She has her reading class this afternoon," Keisha reminded her. Rose nodded. She remembered Alison saying she took special classes once a week after school to help her with her dyslexia. "She's going to join us when she's finished," Keisha went on.

Heather tilted her head as she listened to the music

coming out of the living room. "That's Mozart, isn't it?"

Rose nodded. "He's Grandfather's favorite composer," she said.

"All classical music sounds alike to me," Keisha admitted as the girls headed into the living room.

"Not to Grandfather," Rose said proudly as the older man stood to greet them. "He can name practically any composer within about three notes."

Her grandfather laughed. "Don't exaggerate, Little Flower," he said, using Rose's nickname. "But I do spend a lot of time listening to music. It would be a shame if I didn't learn at least a little bit about it along the way."

"Do you listen only to classical music?" Megan asked the older man, taking a seat next to him on the sofa. "Or do you like Native American music, too?"

Rose gave Megan a quick glance. "There's more to our people than tribal chants, you know, Megan," she blurted out.

"It's all right, Rose," her grandfather said softly. "Your friends are just curious. How else can they learn but by asking questions?" He put a hand on Megan's arm and smiled at her. "As a matter of fact, I *am* interested in native music. Along with jazz, gospel, salsa, reggae, ragtime, and even some rock and roll."

Megan gave Rose a worried glance. "I didn't mean

anything bad, Rose," she said. "Really."

"That's okay," Rose said. She wished she hadn't said anything to Megan, but she hadn't been able to stop herself. She had taken a lot of teasing in the past because of her heritage. Sometimes it was hard to let that go—even around her new friends.

Just then the doorbell rang. "I'll get it," Rose said, relieved to have an excuse to leave the room.

Alison was standing on the doorstep, hopping from foot to foot with excitement. "Hi," she greeted Rose. "You'll never believe what I just heard."

"What?" Rose asked.

Alison shook her head so hard her blond ponytail bounced. "Where are the others? I want to tell you all at the same time." She raced ahead of Rose into the house.

Rose closed the door and followed. When she got back to the living room, her grandfather was on his way out. "I'll leave you girls alone now. Have fun with your friends, Little Flower."

Rose sat down on the floor next to Heather.

Alison was perched on the edge of the easy chair. "On my way to reading class today, I ran into the principal," she began. "He was showing a new teacher around the building. A music teacher."

"But we already have a music teacher," Megan said.

"Right," Alison said. "But we don't have a choir director!" She sat back in the big chair, looking pleased with herself.

Heather looked confused. "Why would we? We don't have a choir."

"Not yet," Alison said meaningfully.

Keisha gasped. "Are you saying what I think you're saying? There's going to be a school choir? Count me in!" Keisha was a member of her church choir and had a strong singing voice.

"Me too," Heather said enthusiastically. "What about you, Rose? Are you as musical as your grandfather?"

Rose smiled. "I like to sing. But I've never been in a choir before."

"This one will be a blast," Alison said. She grinned at Rose, then glanced around at the other girls. "We're all going to try out, right?"

"We have to try out?" Megan said. "What do we have to do?"

Try out? Rose felt her face freeze as she waited for Alison's answer.

Alison shrugged dismissively. "It's no big deal. All we have to do is get up in front of the group and sing a few lines of a song. You know, so the director will know if we're sopranos or altos or whatever."

Rose gulped. She wasn't shy. And she was almost never afraid to speak her mind, no matter who was listening. But for some reason, the thought of singing *by herself* in front of an audience made her knees go weak and her throat go dry.

Rose looked at her friends, wondering if they were nervous about tryouts, too. It certainly didn't appear that way.

"Just think how much fun we'll have being in the choir together," Heather was saying.

"It does sound neat," Megan agreed. "But I'm not an expert singer like Keisha." She grinned. "And I've heard Ali sing. She could use some practice, too. Let's get together this weekend and rehearse."

For a second, Rose felt hopeful. Maybe if she practiced with the other girls they could help her. Maybe she could try out.

Then she pictured herself alone onstage again, and shuddered. There was no way she could do it.

"Good idea," Keisha said, laughing as Alison stuck out her tongue at Megan. "Can everybody come to my house tomorrow?"

Megan, Alison, and Heather nodded. But Rose shook her head. "I don't think so," she said.

"Oh. How about Sunday, then?" Keisha suggested.

Rose hesitated. Megan, Keisha, Alison, and Heather still didn't know her very well. They probably wouldn't understand why she was so worried about singing in front of a big group.

Not knowing what else to do, Rose forced a smile. "The choir sounds like a great time," she said, avoiding her friends' eyes. "But you guys should go ahead and try out without me. I don't really have time for a new activity."

Her friends looked surprised. But Rose barely noticed. Instead, she saw Grandfather's face and heard his voice in her mind:

Have fun with your friends, Little Flower.

Could Heather, Megan, Alison, and Keisha really be her friends if she couldn't tell them her secret?

Chapter

Two

ASKING
FOR HELP

That evening, Rose sat at the kitchen table long after the rest of her family had finished eating dinner, poking at the crumbs on her plate with a carrot stick. She was still thinking about the choir tryouts and the way she'd acted around her friends. Heather and Alison had tried to talk her into joining, while Megan had just looked at her uncertainly, as if she was trying to figure out if Rose was telling the truth. And Keisha—well, Rose wasn't sure exactly what Keisha had thought of her flimsy excuse.

You should have just been honest with them, Rose told herself. They would have understood.

But deep down Rose was convinced that her new friends would never understand why she was so troubled about the tryouts. They would think she was acting weird or something. Maybe they wouldn't even want to hang around with her anymore. Rose would be really upset if that happened. She loved being a part of the Magic Attic Club.

The next afternoon Rose stared out the living room window. Her friends were meeting at that very moment at Keisha's house, but Rose wouldn't be joining them.

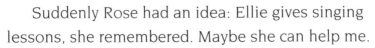

Beyond the treetops in the yard, something caught her eye—the top of her friend Ellie Goodwin's new weather vane.

Suddenly Rose had an idea: Ellie gives singing lessons, she remembered. Maybe she can help me.

Moments later Rose was standing on the porch of Ellie's rambling old Victorian house. Before she could knock on the door, it swung open.

"Rose!" Ellie exclaimed, looking surprised. A smile crinkled the corners of the woman's bright blue eyes.

"Hi, Ellie," Rose greeted her. "Can I talk to you about something?"

Ellie glanced at her watch, then at Rose. "Of course, dear. But I'm afraid I was just running out to the store. I need to get back before my next student arrives."

"Oh." Rose felt a wave of disappointment wash over her. "Never mind," she mumbled. "It's no big deal."

Ellie reached out and pulled her inside. "Don't be silly," she said firmly. "Come on in. I was just going to suggest that you go up to the attic for awhile. We can talk as soon as my student leaves."

Rose instantly felt better. She should have known Ellie wouldn't let her down. After Ellie had let herself out of the house, Rose looked around the wide entry hall. There was no sign of Monty, Ellie's white terrier, and Rose guessed that the dog must be sleeping. She made her way across the hall to a round table that held a small silver box. Opening the box carefully, she took out a golden key.

Soon Rose was on her way up to Ellie's cedar-scented attic. It was bright and airy and filled with all sorts of interesting things that Ellie had brought back from her travels—clothes and trinkets and oddities from every corner of the world. Rose looked around and smiled as she felt her problems drift away in anticipation of another wonderful adventure.

Although she had known Ellie for several years, Rose had only recently discovered the secret of the attic. Alison, Heather, Keisha, and Megan had taken her there and shown her the steamer trunk and mahogany wardrobe full of costumes. Whenever any of the girls put on one of the costumes and then looked in the gilt–framed mirror in the room, she was whisked away to another time and place. After their first adventure, the other four girls had decided to form the Magic Attic Club. Now Rose was a member, too.

Rose lifted the heavy lid of the old trunk and started sifting through the contents. She saw a mint green ballgown and a brightly patterned swimsuit. When she lifted the swimsuit to get a better look, a flash of magenta caught her eye. Dropping the swimsuit on the oriental rug at her feet, she reached for the magenta outfit.

22

First came a cutaway jacket. Its sequined collar and lapels sparkled in the light pouring through the attic windows as Rose held it up. Beneath the jacket was a carefully folded pair of tuxedo pants the same color and a white sleeveless blouse with luxurious ruffles all down the front. Last of all she found a matching sequined top hat and cummerbund.

"This must be some kind of stage costume," Rose whispered, touching the ruffles on the blouse. They rustled and crinkled under her hand. She could just imagine how the shiny fabric and sequins would glow under bright theater lights.

She quickly changed into the outfit. The top hat settled perfectly over her long, thick, dark hair, and she hurried over to look at herself in the mirror.

"Wow," she murmured to her own reflection, as it began to blur. "I look like a real performer now."

Chapter
Three

PETER PRESTO, MASTER MAGICIAN

The next thing Rose knew, she was standing in a large, sunny room bustling with people. Several men and women were gathered near a makeshift stage at one end of the room, and cameras and sound equipment were scattered everywhere. Rock music played softly from a portable radio at the far end of the room. Outside the window she caught a glimpse of an ancient-looking fortress high on top of a hill. But she didn't look out the window for long. There was too much happening inside.

"Check those lights!" yelled a man with a clipboard, racing past her toward a tangle of bulbs and wires lying on the floor nearby.

"Are the speakers ready?" shouted someone else. "Make sure those wires don't get crossed again, or heads will roll! And it won't just be part of the act!"

Rose guessed that she had come upon a rehearsal in full swing. It was always a little disconcerting to suddenly find herself in a new place, but at least this one didn't seem too strange. Most of the people were dressed

in jeans or other casual modern clothes. And nobody
paid attention to Rose's outfit.

She took a few steps closer to the stage, where a tall,
slim woman in her early thirties had just stepped forward.
The woman wore a silvery leotard and a shimmering
white cloak. Her blond hair was pulled on top of her head
and held by a silver tiara decorated with beads and
feathers. As Rose watched, the young woman held up a
dainty silver purse and opened the clasp. She reached
inside and pulled out—a live dove!

Rose gasped as the bird fluttered its snowy wings. The
woman set the dove on a scrolled golden perch, then
reached into the purse again and pulled out another
dove, and another, and still another.

Rose couldn't believe her eyes. The handbag was too
small for even one live bird to fit inside, let alone four. It
had to be magic. And it was incredible. She had never
been this close to a magic act. "Cool," she murmured,
hardly noticing the other people who were rushing
around on every side.

Rose continued to watch as the woman picked up all
four doves and dramatically handed them, one by one, to
a stocky, gray-haired man dressed in a crisp black tuxedo
and a red-lined cape. His hands and hers flashed in a
perfect rhythm as one bird after another was transferred

from the perch to the man's shoulders and arms. Soon all the doves were perched quietly on the man, looking very striking against his black sleeves. He nodded briskly. Rose waited for him to make the doves disappear or something. Instead he turned and handed the birds to a bearded man in jeans, who grabbed a large wire cage and gently pushed them inside.

"Okay, that bit should be fine," the gray-haired man called out. He had a loud voice that carried easily over the commotion in the room. "Nicely done, Karla," he added to the pretty blond woman in the leotard. "The new bird seems okay. We'll do it right after the levitation act as scheduled."

Karla nodded, then looked down to brush a stray feather from her costume. Meanwhile, the man had turned and spotted Rose.

"You must be Rose," he boomed out, jumping down from the stage. Before Rose could react, he grabbed her hand and shook it vigorously. His tuxedo smelled faintly of smoke and chemicals, along with the more pleasant scent of flowers. "I'm glad to meet you," the magician said. "Thanks for stepping in at the last minute like this. Ready to start rehearsing your part?"

Rose nodded uncertainly. She had no idea what he expected her to rehearse, but her friends had said that

Ellie's mirror never let them down during an adventure. When the time came, she would know what to do. At least she hoped so.

"Ready when you are," Rose replied.

The man nodded. "Great," he said. "But first—have you seen this yet?" He pulled a flyer out of his pocket and handed it to her with a smile.

Rose took the flyer. It showed a picture of the man holding a dove in one hand and a top hat in the other. "Peter Presto, Master Magician," the ad read. "Be amazed, be awed, be astounded as he performs his greatest tricks live from Salzburg." Then, big letters across the bottom blared, "Featuring the dramatic Escape from the Killer Bees, performed for the first time anywhere!"

"Tonight's the night," Peter Presto said. "Live TV. Everyone in Europe will be watching us." Suddenly his smile faded and he gave Rose an anxious glance. "That reminds me—we'd better start your rehearsal. If there are any problems, I want to know about them sooner rather than later." He sighed, rubbing his hands together nervously. "I still can't believe my other assistant came down with the flu now of all times," he muttered.

"Don't worry," Rose said. "You can count on me."

"I hope so," Peter said in an uncertain voice. "Stay here. I'll get Karla."

Rose watched him go. She couldn't help feeling a twinge of irritation at his doubtful tone. He almost seemed to be assuming she was going to mess up the rehearsal. But then she shook off the thought. She was being too sensitive, just as her grandfather was always saying she was.

Peter soon returned with the blond woman, Karla, and introduced her to Rose. "Karla has been my second-in-command for years," the magician said. "I couldn't do the show without her."

"Nice to meet you, Rose," Karla said with an open, friendly smile. "I'm glad you're here. We can really use your help."

"Thanks," Rose said. She liked the woman already.

"Okay, let's get started," Peter said briskly. "We'll start out with the floating trick, then move on to the one where I saw you both in half and switch your feet."

What? Rose felt the color drain from her face.

Karla laughed. "Don't worry, Rose. At least you don't have to get in the cage with the killer bees like I do." She gestured at a glass and metal contraption in the wings. It consisted of two glass cages, each about the size of a phone booth. They were linked together by a tube with a small door at each end. One cage was empty. The other was literally buzzing with what looked like several

30

thousand very large, very active
bees.

Rose gulped. "You said I
don't have to get into the
cage, right?"

Peter and Karla laughed again.

"That's right," Peter said. "And
after seeing those bees, catching bullets in your teeth will
seem like a piece of cake!"

"What?" Rose was horrified.

Karla gave Peter a playful shove. "Stop teasing her,"
she ordered. She winked at Rose. "Don't worry. It's just
old magician humor. Nobody catches bullets in their
teeth anymore."

For the next hour, Rose practiced all sorts of tricks.
She learned to make a card appear in the right place by
arranging the cards ahead of time and tricking the
audience into thinking she was shuffling the deck. She
learned to pull a rabbit out of a hat, perform a cup and
ball trick, and make a coin disappear by hiding it under
several colorful silk scarves. Rose also practiced her role
in some of the more complicated tricks, which involved
using a royal blue trunk decorated with silver stars.
Once Peter showed her how the trunk's false bottom

worked, she could figure out the secret behind most of the tricks.

Rose had a great time learning the magic tricks. But she wasn't sure that Peter was having fun. He seemed worried the entire time.

"Nothing will go wrong, Peter," Karla said to him at last. "We've been through every trick twice now, and Rose is a natural. The show will be great—you'll see."

Peter nodded slowly, but he still seemed unconvinced. "I won't completely relax until it's all over," he admitted. "This live TV show is the biggest thing I've done in my whole career. One mistake, and poof!" He waved his hands dramatically. "My career will disappear like magic."

Karla rolled her eyes. "Come on, Rose," she said. "We'd better get out of here while we can. Otherwise, we'll spend the next six hours rehearsing with Mr. Worrywart. Have you seen much of Salzburg yet?"

Rose shook her head. So that's where I am, she said to herself. Salzburg, Austria. "I haven't seen any of it," she said eagerly.

"Good." Karla smiled. "Then let's get out there and do some sightseeing."

Karla and Rose changed into jeans and sweaters and began strolling down the twisting, roughly paved streets of the city. Karla pointed out interesting sights as they walked. Rose sometimes had a hard time talking to new people, but Karla was so friendly that she felt comfortable with her immediately.

Neatly painted old-fashioned buildings towered over the narrow streets on both sides, and metal signs hanging over the doors identified the shops and restaurants within. Salzburg seemed more like a small town from the past than a modern city. Almost never out of view on its hilltop high above the city was the huge stone fortress Rose had noticed earlier.

"They call the fortress Hohensalzburg," Karla told her. "It's more than nine hundred years old. That's where our show is tonight."

"Really?" Rose said. "Peter didn't mention that."

Karla chuckled. "No surprise there," she said. "This close to showtime Peter hardly has time to eat or sleep, let alone talk to people about anything except what he thinks they need to know. And this show...well..." She let her voice trail off.

"What?" Rose asked as they rounded a corner and found themselves on a charming tree-lined street beside a wide river.

"This show is probably the most important one Peter has ever done," Karla said. "He's already got an international reputation, but this could really make him famous. Especially after he performs the bee trick."

Rose couldn't help shuddering as she remembered those buzzing, circling, tireless bees—killer bees, according to the poster Peter had shown her. "Exactly what happens during this bee trick, anyway?" she asked.

Karla smiled and flung out her arms. "Ladies and gentlemen," she exclaimed. "You won't bee-lieve your eyes! Observe this hive of buzzing bees. This very colony once stung four campers almost to the point of death because they happened to walk too close to their hive. Now Peter Presto's lovely assistant will risk life and limb by standing in this adjoining glass cage and holding back the stinging demons with the strength of her will." She gasped, putting her hands to her face in mock horror. "Oh, no! The bees are too much for her. They're swarming over her. Oh, dear—it may be too late..."

A few tourists with cameras applauded politely from a nearby street corner. Karla gave them a little wave as they snapped her picture. "Watch us on live TV tonight and find out what happens next," she called to them.

Rose was eager to hear how the trick ended. "What does happen next?" she asked once the tourists had wandered off.

Karla winked. "Peter runs backstage, pretending it's a

big disaster. Meanwhile the bees are swarming in the cage so nobody can see what's going on. Then smoke fills the cage and the bees head back into their hive. The next thing the audience sees is Peter, dressed in full beekeeping attire, waving at them from inside the cage where the assistant was just standing. Someone opens a closet at the back of the stage and there's the assistant sitting inside, calmly sipping tea—with honey, of course."

Rose laughed. It sounded like a great trick to her, dramatic and funny. She was even more impressed after Karla carefully explained how it was really done.

"Just don't tell Peter I told you," Karla said with a wink. "He'll have my head. And you've seen those saws he has!"

Rose laughed. "The secret's safe with me. I can't wait to see the trick tonight," she replied. "By the way, I have another very important question for you."

"What?" Karla asked. "Some other trick of the trade you're curious about?"

"Nope." Rose rubbed her stomach and smiled. "When's lunch? All that magic really works up an appetite."

Chapter

Four

ILLUSIONS AND SHOWMANSHIP

arla led the way to a small café called Café Musik. When they were seated at a table in the dark, cool restaurant, Rose decided to ask another question. "Why is Peter so nervous about this show?" she asked. "I mean, I know it's on live TV and everything, but still…"

Karla sighed. "Worrying is Peter's hobby. He never trusts that anything is going to go the way it should, even though it always does. I've been working with him for almost ten years now, and I've never seen him flub a trick during a show."

Rose nodded. She was glad that he hadn't just been worried about her abilities. "He's that good?" she asked.

"He's the best," Karla said firmly. "And don't be upset if he doesn't seem to trust you at first. It's only because you're new." She rolled her eyes. "He wouldn't tell me any of his secrets until I'd been with him over a year."

Rose sipped her water while she thought that over. On the one hand, she couldn't blame Peter for expecting people to prove themselves before he trusted them. Rose could be that way herself sometimes. Still, she couldn't help thinking he should at least give her a chance before assuming the worst.

A waitress brought them cups of tea and a plate of flaky pastries. Rose mixed sugar into her tea and took a dessert. "When did you decide you wanted to be a magician?" she asked Karla.

Karla smiled. "I've been

driving my friends and family crazy with my tricks for as long as I can remember."

"Really?" Rose said. "What kind of tricks did you do when you were a kid?"

"Oh, all kinds of things," Karla said. "But I have to admit, I didn't learn it all on my own. My grandfather is one of the best amateur magicians ever. He still helps me with new tricks sometimes. Just don't tell Peter that. He thinks it's all my own natural talent."

Rose laughed. "Is your grandfather coming to the show tonight?" she asked. "I'd love to meet him."

Karla shook her head. Her expression became sad. "Gramps can't make it to this show," she said softly. "He's in the hospital. His doctors say he's probably going to need an operation soon."

"Oh. I'm sorry." Rose wasn't sure what else to say.

But a moment later, Karla brightened. "I can show you a couple of my tricks that Gramps taught me," she offered.

"Sure," Rose said eagerly.

"Okay. But first, let me go call my mom," Karla said. "I want to check on how Gramps is doing. Back in a sec."

Rose sipped her tea while she waited. "Did you reach your mother?" she asked when Karla returned to the table.

"My mom wasn't there," Karla explained, looking worried. "I guess I'll have to try again later, after the show." Then she took a deep breath and smiled at Rose. "Ready to be amazed?" she asked. "Now I'm going to show you why cats and dogs don't get along."

Rose noticed a young tourist couple with a small boy sitting at the next table. All three of them turned their heads to watch what Karla was doing.

Karla didn't pay any attention to them. She picked up a clean ashtray from the center of the table and carefully poured water into it from her glass. "I don't know why, but cats and dogs hate each other. Say this salt is a bunch of dogs. Watch them play!" She grabbed the salt shaker and shook some salt into the water, then stirred it with her finger so the grains seemed to race around like playful dogs.

Rose giggled. The little boy at the next table was watching closely, too.

"Now if salt is dogs, guess what cats are?" Karla said.

"Pepper!" called out the little boy. He spoke English with a British accent.

Karla smiled at him and his parents. "That's right, young man," she said. She sprinkled some pepper into the dish. "Here are the cats. But watch what happens when I try to make them play with the dogs." Again, she put one finger into the water. Before she could swirl it around, the black dots of pepper seemed to spring away, rushing to the edge of the dish.

The little boy cried out in amazement, and even Rose gasped.

"See?" Karla finished with a shrug. "They just don't get along."

The British couple and their son applauded. Then they returned to their food, though Rose noticed that the little boy kept sneaking awed glances at Karla.

"How did you do that?" Rose asked quietly.

Karla grinned. "All I needed was a little preparation, and science took care of the rest." She held up the index fingers on each hand. "I really did call my mother just now. But I also stopped by the restroom and rubbed soap on the end of this finger." She wiggled the finger on her right hand. "When I stirred the salt, I used my left finger. The second time, with the pepper, I stirred with the soapy one. A soapy film was created on the surface of the water, and that's what made the pepper 'run' from my finger." She winked at Rose. "And no matter how many times that little boy tries it at home, he'll never get it to work without knowing about the soap."

Rose laughed. "It's so simple when you know the trick behind it."

"A lot of magic is," Karla said. "Let me show you something else you can do with a salt shaker." She picked up the shaker in both hands and started rubbing it all over while she continued to talk. "Once you know the physical principles, the key is to know how to make people believe in what you're doing."

Out of the corner of her eye, Rose saw that the family at the next table was watching again.

Karla noticed, too. "Once when I was in India," she said in a louder voice, "I learned the secret of defying the laws of gravity. What I'm doing now is rearranging the molecules of this salt shaker so it will levitate." After a few more seconds of rubbing, Karla grasped the shaker by its top and raised her hand a few inches. Then, slowly, one by one, she removed her fingers. Soon the shaker was suspended below the tip of her longest finger, seeming to float in thin air.

"Take your hand away!" the little boy cried.

Karla shook her head solemnly. "I can't do that," she told him. "Otherwise the salt shaker would float right up to the ceiling. I'd better fix it now before the waitress gets angry." She rubbed the shaker again for a few seconds, then set it back in the middle of the table with a flourish. Once again, the little boy and his parents applauded.

"Do another one," the boy begged.

"Sorry," Karla said with a smile. "If you want to see more magic, you'll have to watch our show on TV tonight." She told the family about the live special that was being filmed at the old stone fortress.

"I'll watch," the little boy said earnestly. "I promise."

"Wonderful," Karla said. She leaned over and plucked a coin out of the air behind the boy's ear. She gave him the coin, stood and bowed as the whole family applauded, and sat down.

"Okay, I know how you did the first trick," Rose said

with a giggle. "But what about the floating salt shaker?"

Karla checked to be sure the family wasn't watching. "That one required one prop," she said quietly. She reached into her lap and picked up a toothpick. "While I was pretending to 'rearrange the molecules,' I was actually working the end of this into one of the holes on the top of the salt shaker," she said. "Then I just held onto the other end with my thumb, which was tucked behind my hand where you couldn't see it. You couldn't see the toothpick, either, because it was behind my finger."

Rose laughed. "That's great," she exclaimed. She was starting to understand why Karla loved magic so much. It was really fun to see people's amazement and to make them smile. "I can't wait to try that trick on my friends sometime."

"All it takes is practice," Karla said. "And a bit of showmanship, of course."

Someone in the back of the restaurant had just switched on a radio. Classical music started playing softly from a set of speakers in the corner. Rose immediately recognized the piece. "Hey, I know this," she said. "It's Mozart."

Karla chuckled. "Of course it is. They play it everywhere around here. For the tourists, you know."

"What do you mean?" Rose tipped her head back to

drain the last of her tea from the cup.

"Didn't you know?" Karla looked surprised. "Mozart was born here in Salzburg. There are statues of him all around the city, and you can almost always find a Mozart concert going on. In fact, there's going to be a Mozart chamber concert following our show tonight."

"Cool," Rose said, thinking about her grandfather.

Karla checked her watch. "Come on. If we hurry, I can show you the house where Mozart was born before we have to get dressed for the show."

As Rose stood up from the table, she couldn't help wishing that her grandfather was there to see it, too.

Chapter

Five

THE BIG SHOW

T wo hours before showtime, Rose had butterflies in her stomach. She and Karla were once again hurrying through the streets of Salzburg. This time, it was almost evening and lights were blinking on in all the old buildings and squares. After visiting the house where Mozart was born, Rose and Karla emerged into an open square near the foot of the hill that held the fortress. Rose had to look almost straight up to see the huge, forbidding stone building far above. "How do we get up there?" she asked. "I hope we don't have to climb."

"Don't worry," Karla said. She pointed to a sign that said *Festungsbahn*. "We'll take the train."

When they got closer, Rose could see a sort of tram waiting at the base of the hill. She and Karla joined the people waiting to board, and soon they were all rising swiftly along the track.

"This is fun," Rose said. "What did people do before this train was invented?"

Karla grinned. "I don't know," she said. "But they've had a train running here since 1892. The first one was powered with water instead of electricity."

The ride was brief, and soon Rose and Karla were making their way through the fortress to the hall where the performance was to take place. Along the way, Rose caught glimpses of fascinating-looking rooms and passageways. At one point Karla paused long enough to point out a fantastic view of Salzburg through a narrow window. The river below sparkled in the light of the setting sun.

"Almost there," Karla said after leading Rose down a few more passageways. "Here is our dressing room." Rose and Karla changed back into their stage costumes with long coats over them to guard against the chill in the fortress. But the cool evening air wasn't the only thing making Rose shiver. She was about to take part in a magic act on live TV! Rose felt her stomach jump again with excitement.

On their way to the stage, they passed a small room, and when Rose peeked in she saw a group of kids about her age assembling musical instruments.

Karla noticed them, too. "That's the chamber orchestra that will be playing right after our act. They're some of the best young musicians in Austria."

"There you are!" a voice boomed out from down the hall. It was Peter. He hurried toward them, resplendent in his tuxedo and a bright red cummerbund that matched the lining of his cloak.

Just then a stagehand rushed up to them. "There's a phone message for you, Karla," he said. "In the dressing room. It sounded pretty urgent."

"Thanks," Karla told the man. She glanced at Peter, looking anxious. "I'd better go see what that's about."

The magician nodded, and Karla hurried off in the opposite direction. Peter and Rose continued down the hall, then turned off into a large room. At first it appeared to be filled wall-to-wall with TV cameras and equipment.

Then Rose saw a stage that stretched across one end of the room. Several dozen people were seated on folding chairs in front of it.

"Our audience," Peter whispered. "It looks pretty small, but that's all they could fit in the room." He waved one hand at the TV cameras. "Besides, our real audience tonight is out there. Millions of people, if we're lucky."

Rose felt nervous about appearing before such a huge audience, but she felt a flutter of anticipation as well. She couldn't wait for the show to start.

"Ladies and gentlemen!" a voice cried. "For your entertainment this evening, the mystical wonders of Peter Presto, Master Magician!"

Rose gulped. Nervousness about appearing onstage was the least of her problems now. Karla still hadn't returned.

"What should I do?" Rose whispered to a stagehand as Peter strode out in front of the cameras.

The man shrugged, looking worried. "Do you know how to do Karla's first trick?" he asked. "It's the one with the doves."

Rose nodded. Karla had told her that the dove trick worked just like the rabbit trick she had learned earlier.

"You'd better step in, then," the stagehand said. "I'll send one of the crew to look for Karla."

With a deep breath, Rose stepped onstage. The audience applauded enthusiastically. Peter looked surprised to see her, but he went on with the dove trick as if nothing were wrong.

It went perfectly. Rose's hands seemed to know exactly what to do. After her part was finished, she stepped back. While Peter finished up the dove trick, her eyes flicked to the bees' glass-walled hive sitting onstage.

Rose wasn't the only one watching the bees. People in the audience kept shooting glances at the glass contraption, too, and whispering to each other. The bees played their part well, buzzing loudly and creating a constant noise.

After the dove trick was finished, Rose bowed. For his next trick, Peter began pulling the multicolored scarves and other props out of the royal blue trunk.

Rose hurried backstage, glancing frantically around for Karla. As she peeked out into the hall, the stagehand hurried toward her.

"Bad news," he said grimly. "Karla's grandfather took a turn for the worse. He's going into surgery, and Karla already left for the airport. There was only one flight that would get her there in time."

Rose gasped. She could hardly believe that this was happening. Poor Karla! Her grandfather meant so much to her.

Then Rose realized she should feel sorry for Peter, too, and for herself. How would they ever get through the show without Karla?

The stagehand seemed to guess what she was thinking. "Don't worry, Rose," he said. "Karla said that she's sure that you can handle her parts in all the other tricks."

"All of them?" Rose asked in a shaky voice. She pictured those bees, buzzing hungrily in their glass cage. "Even the bee trick?"

The stagehand nodded. "Karla seemed to think you could do it."

Rose didn't have any more time to think about it. She had to get back onstage.

Rose lay down on a table and let Peter drape a sheet over her. The magician still didn't know about Karla, but there was no chance to tell him.

The audience gasped in amazement as Rose levitated several feet above the table, following Peter's magic wand. Then he started to lower the wand. As he did, Rose was lowered, too. And Peter himself started to float into the air! Soon he was "standing" several feet above the floor, while Rose was once again lying on the table. The audience laughed and burst into applause.

As soon as the trick was over, Rose quickly whispered

the news to Peter. His expression didn't change until the TV director yelled, "Clear! We're in commerical, folks."

Then Peter turned to Rose. "What did you just say?"

Rose repeated her news. She had to jog to keep up with him as he hurried offstage.

"Oh no, it's her grandfather?" Peter said, looking concerned. "What's wrong with him?" Then he seemed to remember that they were in the middle of a show. "Wait a minute. Where did she go?"

Rose explained about the flight. "But Karla said I should just step in and do her parts," she explained. The more she thought about it, the more certain she was that she could do it. Well, except maybe for that bee trick...

"This is a disaster," Peter moaned. "These tricks take a lot of practice. You're good, Rose, but—"

"I can do it, Peter," Rose cut in firmly. "You have to let me try."

Peter stopped and gave Rose a thoughtful look. "I don't have a choice," he murmured. "I guess we'll have to see how it goes."

Rose didn't think he sounded very optimistic. I'll show him, she thought determinedly. This show will go perfectly.

The rest of the show went just as well as Rose had hoped. She and Peter kept the audience gasping and giggling. Peter made rabbits do multiplication, caused Rose to disappear and then reappear behind one of the television cameras, and even sawed himself in half, bantering with the audience all along. Rose could tell he was upset about Karla, but no one in the audience would ever have guessed.

Rose was always busy, but she was having a good time, too. All the tricks she had practiced that morning went perfectly, and the ones she did in Karla's place were just as successful.

It was great to hear the enthusiastic response from the live audience, and to know that lots more people all over the continent were enjoying themselves just as much. There were only two worrisome thoughts that occasionally distracted Rose from enjoying the performance. One was concern for Karla's grandfather. The other was nervousness about the bee trick. It was a complicated one, and one that would make or break the entire show. Could she really do it?

Before Rose knew it, it was time for the next-to-last trick of the evening. Peter took off his shoes and asked Rose to handcuff his left ankle to a heavy weight. Then he proceeded to free himself with his right foot while juggling an apple, a throw pillow, a glass vase, and a large curved knife in his hands. At the end he held up his

foot, victorious, and then pretended to
drop the items he was juggling. The
vase landed safely on the pillow,
and the knife sliced the apple
cleanly in two. The audience
burst into applause, and Peter
swept into a deep bow.

Now all that was left was the bee
trick, and the show would be over.

But just before the commercial break, Peter stepped
forward to speak to the audience. "I'm afraid there's been
an unfortunate change in plans," he said. "I hope you
won't be too disappointed. More details after this word
from your sponsors."

Rose, who was watching from the wings, was taken by
surprise. She had no idea what he was talking about.

Peter hurried toward her as soon as the cameras were
off. "I'm sorry, Rose," he said. "You've done magnificently
tonight. Better than I could have hoped. But I can't ask
you to do the bee trick. It's too dangerous. I couldn't
possibly explain it to you in time. I'm going to have to
cancel it."

Rose glanced toward the stage. Suddenly the bees
looked even scarier than they had before. There were
thousands of them in that hive. And each one had its own

sharp stinger.

Should she tell Peter that she already knew how to do the trick?

Six

ACTIONS AND WORDS

Rose took a deep breath. "I can do it, Peter," she said. "Karla explained how the trick works." She knew that she had promised Karla not to tell Peter that. But this was definitely one case where a secret was better not kept.

Peter hardly seemed to hear her. "I should have known this show was a mistake," he muttered. "Live TV! What was I thinking?" He let out a deep sigh. "Well, that's that. Unless Karla missed her flight and shows up back here in the next"—he glanced at his watch—"two minutes, I'll have to tell the audience that the trick is canceled."

"But Peter…" Rose thought the magician was being awfully dramatic about this. "You don't have to cancel," she insisted loudly. "I can do it. Really."

Peter shook his head. "I'm sorry, Rose," he said, his voice a little gentler than before. "This trick can be dangerous if you don't know what you're doing. I can't risk it."

"But I *do* know what I'm doing," Rose said, almost to herself. Peter hadn't even heard her. He was striding back toward center stage. All around her, Rose saw stagehands scurrying out of sight. The commercial break was almost over.

"Thirty seconds, everyone," the director called.

Rose felt her heart sink. She wished Peter wouldn't be so stubborn. She certainly didn't relish the thought of being locked in the cage with those bees, but after what Karla had told her that afternoon, she was sure she could fill in and perform her part perfectly. There was very little danger if you knew exactly what to do, and Rose did. Why couldn't Peter trust her?

"Places, everyone!" the director called urgently. "Five seconds…four…"

Suddenly Rose remembered one of her grandfather's

favorite phrases: Actions speak louder than words. And she knew what she had to do.

Just as the TV cameras started filming again, she raced onto the stage. Peter, who had just opened his mouth to begin his apology, let his jaw hang open in amazement as Rose quickly let herself into the glass cage and flipped the switch to release the bees.

C h a p t e r

Seven

ROSE TO THE RESCUE

Inside the cage, Rose held her breath as the first few bees buzzed in lazily. From this close, the black and yellow insects looked larger than ever. She tried not to notice their stingers, praying that Peter would follow her lead.

Out on the stage, she could hear the master magician through the glass. His voice sounded shaky.

"Ladies and gentlemen, what you see before you is our own lovely Rose, performing as human bug spray for our own colony of killer bees. As you can see, she's holding back the fearsome little critters with the force of her will."

The audience was already murmuring, since the glass cage was filling rapidly with bees even as Peter spoke.

The magician glanced over his shoulder and jumped in surprise. "Oh, no!" he cried fearfully. "It's not working! They're getting through!"

Rose knew it was all part of the act, but the audience gasped, obviously believing that something had gone terribly wrong.

"I've got to get help," Peter said. By this time Rose was completely obscured from the audience's view by a swarm of bees. Peter raced to the back of the stage and flung open a door, revealing a large closet filled with books and papers. "I think there's something in one of these books about beekeeping," he exclaimed to the audience. "Maybe that will tell me how to help poor Rose." He let himself into the closet and closed the door.

By now a few titters were coming from the audience. Rose knew they were wondering what was going on.

The crowd found out a few seconds later. Thick white smoke filled the inside of the glass cage. The bees, eager to escape the hated smoke, buzzed back into their own hive. A white-gloved hand closed the small door behind them and started waving away the smoke. Then a figure stepped out of the cage wearing a white beekeeper's outfit, complete with nylon hood. He pulled off the hood with a flourish, revealing his face. It was Peter.

"Whew!" he cried. "That was close." He strode to the closet door and flung it open, revealing Rose within. The books had disappeared, and the little room now contained only a comfortable chair and a little table, upon which sat a dainty cup of tea—and a huge glass jar of golden honey.

The audience burst into thunderous applause as Peter stepped into the closet and shut the door on Rose and himself. A second later the door opened again, and the two performers emerged. Peter's beekeeper outfit had disappeared, and he took Rose's arm and swung her into a deep bow.

Rose grinned as they bowed again and again I did it, she thought. I saved the show!

The applause seemed to wash over her.

"I guess you had a trick or two up your own sleeve, didn't you, young lady?" Peter whispered to her.

Rose glanced at him out of the corner of her eye. Was he angry with her for disobeying her?

The magician winked. "Don't worry," he murmured. "I know how to admit when I was wrong. And I also know

how to say thank you—you saved my reputation."

Rose grinned as they bowed again. "You're welcome," she whispered back.

Finally the director called, "Cut! We're clear, people. Nice show." He gave a thumbs-up sign to Rose, and she smiled back.

Then she and Peter walked offstage as the stagehands rushed to clear away the props so the musicians could set up for their concert.

"I mean it, you know," Peter said in his normal voice. "I really want to thank you, Rose. You did a fantastic job out there. I'm sorry I didn't believe you could do it. Even if I didn't trust you, I should have known Karla wouldn't ask you to step in if she didn't think you could handle it. She knows her stuff."

An hour later, Rose and Peter were watching the Mozart concert from backstage when a stagehand tapped Peter on the shoulder.

"Karla's on the phone," the man whispered. "She wants to talk to you. Both of you." He smiled at Rose.

Peter and Rose hurried to the dressing room. Peter grabbed the phone first. "Karla!" he exclaimed. "How's your grandfather?"

He held the phone away from his ear so Rose could hear Karla's answer, too.

"He's okay." Karla sounded tired but happy. "He was in pretty bad shape earlier, but the surgery was successful. I got here just as it was ending. Now his doctors say he's going to make a full recovery."

"That's wonderful," Peter said. Rose could tell he meant it. "Just do me a favor, okay?" the magician went on. "Ask your family to try not to have any more emergencies when we're going onstage."

"I already did," Karla said with a laugh. "Listen, Peter, I'm really sorry I ran off like that. But my grandfather—"

"Don't say another word," Peter interrupted. "He's your *grandfather*. Besides, I know he taught you everything you know about magic—except what you've learned from me, of course."

Rose laughed at the astonished gasp that came from the phone. "I guess it's pretty hard to trick a magician," she joked, leaning forward so Karla could hear her.

"Oh, I don't know about that," Peter said. "You tricked me tonight, Rose." He smiled broadly. "And I'm sure glad you did. Here. Karla wants to say hi to you."

Rose took the phone. "Is your grandfather really okay?" she asked.

"Definitely," Karla assured her. "And thanks to you, it sounds like Peter might even forgive me for running off like this."

Rose glanced at the magician. "I think he already has," she said. "Thanks for teaching me all those tricks today. Seeing you make magic with a salt shaker and a dish of water kind of inspired me. I figured if you could make that little boy in the restaurant believe in magic with just that stuff, I should be able to do it with Peter and all those props."

Karla laughed. "I'm glad," she said. "And thanks again—from me and my gramps—for taking over."

"You're welcome." Rose said good-bye to Karla and handed the phone back to Peter. "Here. I'm sure you two want to talk. I'll leave you alone."

Rose stepped into the hallway. She turned in the direction of the concert room and listened for one more moment as the magical notes of a Mozart sonata filled the air. Then Rose slipped backstage, where the magician's equipment was waiting to be moved back to his hotel. She wandered around until she found the piece she was looking for—a large funhouse-style mirror. Giving her sequined hat a tap to make sure it was settled firmly on her head, she looked into the mirror.

Chapter

Eight

A SONG
FOR ROSE

Back in Ellie's attic, Rose changed into her own clothes and carefully placed the magician's costume back in the trunk. She locked the attic door with the golden key and hurried downstairs.

She could hear voices as she reached the first floor. It sounded as though Ellie was saying good-bye to her student.

As soon as she heard the front door close, Rose joined Ellie in the front hall. "Well, hello," Ellie greeted her. "Did you have a nice time?"

Rose grinned. "Did I ever!" she exclaimed, following Ellie into the sitting room.

Ellie sat on the long sofa and patted the cushion beside her. "You wanted to talk to me about something?"

Rose took a seat—and a deep breath. It wasn't easy for her to confide her feelings, even to Ellie. "I think I need your help, Ellie," she blurted out. Rose told Ellie about the choir auditions at school. "The thought of trying out—singing onstage *all by myself*—scares me to death. But I didn't know how to tell my friends that. None of them seemed scared at all. I'm afraid they'll think there's something wrong with me if they find out."

Ellie listened quietly until she was finished. Then she nodded slowly. "I see," she said. "Rose, did I ever tell you about the time I sang for the Queen of England?"

Rose's eyes widened. She knew that Ellie had been a performer before retiring and moving to this house to give lessons. But she didn't know she had sung for the queen. "You did?" she exclaimed.

"I did," Ellie said. "And let me tell you, before I went into that room, I was so terribly nervous that I was sure I was going to faint dead away."

"Really?" Rose said. She couldn't imagine calm, confident Ellie ever being nervous about anything. "Was it the first time you ever sang for someone important?"

Ellie shook her head and smiled. "Oh my, no. It wasn't even the first time I'd sung for royalty." She patted Rose on the knee. "You see, I get nervous every time I sing for an audience—to this very day. It's perfectly natural, and nothing to be ashamed of. You just have to learn to manage your fear, that's all."

"How do you do that?" Rose asked uncertainly. She still could hardly believe that Ellie got nervous. But it made her feel a little better. She wasn't the only one who got scared.

"If you want to try out for the choir with your friends, I'll teach you some tricks to help you relax," Ellie said. "Why don't you stop by tomorrow and we'll practice some of them."

Rose nodded. "I'd like that. Thanks. "

"You're welcome." Ellie smiled at her. "It's always nice to have someone else on your team—or a friendly face in the audience."

The doorbell rang. Ellie went to answer it and returned to the sitting room a moment later followed by Alison, Heather, Keisha, and Megan.

"Hi, Rose," Heather said. "Your grandfather told us you were here."

"We wanted to talk to you about something," Keisha

began, speaking slowly and tentatively. "We don't want to try to talk you into doing anything you really don't want to do, but—"

Alison broke in impatiently. "We want you to be in the choir with us," she said quickly.

Rose glanced at Ellie, then back at her friends. Now that she had one person on her team, maybe she could recruit four more. "I guess I should talk to you guys about that," she said. "You see, the real reason I didn't want to try out is because…I was afraid." She did her best to explain her fear of singing alone onstage.

"I know how you feel," Megan said, sitting down and putting an arm around Rose's shoulders. "I'm pretty nervous about trying out, too. I know the only way I can do it is if all of my friends are cheering me on."

"Me, too," Heather put in. "We'll help you any way we can—if you do want to try out, that is."

Rose couldn't believe her ears. Her friends did understand. They didn't think she was weird at all. She looked from one friendly face to the other. All of a sudden, she realized how silly she had been not to trust them. It was even sillier than Peter Presto's not trusting her to do the bee trick.

Thinking about Peter made her smile. She couldn't wait to tell the others about her magical adventure in Austria. She had learned more than magic tricks while she was there. She had learned that magicians had to keep secrets from their audiences; that was what made their acts work. But now she also knew that for a friendship to work, the opposite was true. Friends had to trust each other, secrets and all.

"Of course I want to be in the choir," Rose said happily. She still felt nervous about the tryouts, but that was okay. Her friends would help her through it. "Now come on. Let's go practice."

Diary

Dear Diary,

Guess what? I survived choir tryouts!

It was really scary, and when I first stood up I wasn't sure I was going to be able to do it, even after all of Ellie's help. She taught me a lot of breathing exercises and stuff to keep me calm beforehand. But as soon as it was my turn, it felt like about a million butterflies — no, better make that killer bees —were on the loose in my stomach.

But then I looked out at the audience, and I saw my friends sitting right there in the front row. They all held up their hands, and I could see that they all had their fingers crossed for me! That made me feel a lot better, and suddenly I was able to start singing, just like magic!

Speaking of magic, my friends loved hearing

about Peter Presto and my adventure in Salzburg. They loved the magic tricks Karla taught me even more. I'm still trying to decide if I should show them how they're really done — some secrets are fun to keep!

Being part of Peter Presto's magic act was really exciting. I think being in the choir will be almost as great. I can't wait until our first rehearsal!

Until next time,

P.S. As far as I'm concerned, Keisha and Alison can have all the solos!

JOIN THE MAGIC ATTIC CLUB!

You can enjoy every adventure of the Magic Attic Club just by reading all the books. And there's more!

You can have a whole world of fun with the dolls, outfits, and accessories that are based on the books. And since Alison, Keisha, Heather, and Megan can wear one another's clothes, you can relive their adventures, or create new ones of your own!

To join the Magic Attic Club, just fill out this postcard and drop it in the mail, or call toll free **1-800-775-9272**. We'll send you a **free** membership kit

including a membership card, a poster, stickers, postcards, and a catalog with all four dolls.

With your first purchase of a doll, you'll also receive your own key to the attic. And it's FREE!

- -

Yes, I want to join the Magic Attic Club!

My name is _____

My address is _____

City _____ State _____ Zip _____

Birth date _____ Parent's Signature _____

966

And send a catalog to my friend, too!

My friend's name is _____

Address _____

City _____ State _____ Zip _____

967

If someone has already used the postcard from
this book and you would like a free Magic Attic Club
catalog, just send your full name and address to:

Magic Attic Club
866 Spring Street
P.O. Box 9712
Portland, ME 04104-9954

Or call toll free
1-800-775-9272

Code: 968